THE BOOK OF

TRANSPARENCIES

Jefferson Navicky

KERNPUNKT ● PRESS

Cover Art: [Nude boy in rocky landcape above water, arms raised, silhouette] from the Library of Congress Prints and Photographs Division Washington, D.C. 20540 USA
Book Design: Jesi Buell

1st Printing: 2018

ISBN-13 978-0-9972924-9-7

KERNPUNKT Press
701 State Route 12B
Hamilton, New York 13346

www.kernpunktpress.com

For Sarah

Transparency is full of holes.

❈

I began to deal and it seemed impossible to me that I could ever have a life apart from Plaza Santa Lupe   the flat slip of playing cards   the homely click of ice cubes steeped in vermouth like a clock hand stuck in its groove

❈

In the library of the community college where I taught English Composition and Speech in 2005, I came upon a slim anomaly of a book with an ash blue cover entitled The Book of Transparencies by William Bolzebados. I regularly had time between classes and because I was an adjunct with no office for myself, I often searched through the shelves at random, selected a book and read a few sections. This was how I discovered the book. It was a collection of vignettes, poems, letters, drawings and notes about Bolzebados's relationship with the artist Cleo Barnes written in a thinly veiled autobiographical voice that—there is no other way to say this—finished my thoughts so completely and in a voice so close to mine that I began to wonder if I had written the book in some forgotten past life. Aside from the prose for which I held the aforementioned affinity despite certain indulgent romantic flourishes, I was drawn to the lack of punctuation that lent the text a ghostly quality of floating or existing tenuously, riddled with holes. I especially appreciated the drawing of the single wooden chair whose legs splayed impossibly across the inside back cover, a slip in perspective like a young deer attempting to stand for the first time. I was able to read the book in one sitting, using my entire two hour break between classes to consume the book in a stone skip reading where I consciously bounced along its surface relishing the thought that I would soon have to return and pay closer attention to its depths. When I finished, a line remained in my head: "On your best walks in the city, you were able to feel you were nowhere, alone in a room firing a pistol into the base of a bare white wall." I held this line in my memory, writing it on napkins and in letters for weeks before I finally began my search.

*

I tried to move and recover but her scent came roaring back like a train exiting a tunnel and I awoke without memory of the terror   only the sharp fading scent of metal and even that vanished before I hardly knew it was there   a thief disappearing around a corner I lay in bed alone   unable to recognize my surroundings but convinced that if I moved a six-foot seven-inch shadow of a man in the corner of the room would stride out and finish me   I reached out for Cleo but of course she was not there and when I failed to find her body next to me I began to emerge   during those months   before I left for Europe   inexplicable fears whose depths I could not fathom   plagued me   pain and fear far greater than myself   greater than the suffering I'd accumulated in this life and while I didn't know the source the power was undeniable like slipping a knife in because a fist won't fit   my method for coping with this terror   once I was able to situate myself outside the fear   was to walk the city   long winding walks   in the middle of night on my most transensory walks in the city   I was able to feel I was nowhere   lost in my white thoughts that slowly settled into a trance cadence   it was surprisingly easy to traverse the city from end to end on foot in a single night and I found that in a matter of hours I could loop a majority of the city's center   keeping as much as I could to the alleys and the side streets   occasionally walking down the larger thoroughfares of the Gambon or Central or sometimes Broadway to the base of the Memorial Bridge   crossing this bridge was my most elegant traversal   I lost myself in thoughts of the one hundred eighty six men who died in the construction of the cables and stone arches   and the vision of the architect Von Walser   an emigrant from the Black Forest   climbing the cables and shafts himself to evaluate the view from the central tower while his wife and young boy waited at home for him on the apex of the span I fantasized about jumping and what I would hear under water   according to the Kabala the most dangerous place for a man is on a bridge while for a woman it is in childbirth I jump from the bridge in the middle of night while the city spreads out around me in electric clusters but before I do this I will have spent my time in the old slave graveyard   gathering bones and flowers and candles and scraps of paper affixed to graves I will boil the bones and eat them as Tibetans did with dragon bones for their magical strength and healing properties the flowers and candles and flotsam will string along behind me as a tail so when I jump   it will be as a shooting star

I couldn't tell who the speakers were I carefully rose from the bed and   with the help of my stick reached the door perhaps I moved too hurriedly and they heard me because a silence grew outside   silence like a plant putting out tendrils that grew under the door and into the room where I stood it was a silence I did not enjoy and I tore it apart by flinging the door open the orderly who had given me the pea coat stood outside my room   talking sotto voce with another nurse they stopped and I was convinced they were talking about me as I stood in the hallway   indignation rising off me in waves   they turned and left me standing in the middle of the air I wanted to chase after them   shake them by their lapels and shout in their faces but I was in no condition to do any of that I leaned on the derby walking stick my brother brought up from Brooklyn he knew I loved cherry's soft color and grain I could literally feel the insanity leeching up through my pores   a mixture of rage and self-pity   dementia and wistfulness I thought of the whale skeleton interred since 1904 in the Nantucket Whaling Museum the museum staff   when they began to collect the spermaceti   used every available container in the museum from bowls to buckets to a rowboat and they still were only able to collect one hundred gallons of the estimated three hundred in the forehead of the whale   it is intensity rather than calmness I seek   and in the given impulsive moment   in the face of the mind's leakage   is a controlled touch even possible?

❖

Though he was unable to see it, the elaborate cipher of constellations stretched above him as he walked towards Plaza Santa Lupe. He felt the security of his age along the darkened streets, rain coming down. Water trickled off his nose and he remembered water running between her thin wing-like shoulder blades. He walked into a triangular park. Could he become a ruthless dictator that allowed the misery of thousands to ensure the survival of one love? He wanted to return to Santa Lupe by dawn to continue to work on The Book of Transparencies and if the rain lessened he could. He stepped through tiny rivers of mud. The patrol would not be out tonight. Whoever crossed the city in this weather did so at his own peril.

His fingers stroked the smooth rock in his pocket. His eye twitched with recollection, writing letters to his brother from his asylum desk   looking over dew-dropped lawns, dipping fountain pen into ink well   wiping the excess on a napkin from the kitchen, his long looping script filling pages, details of his perambulations through the gardens, birds he saw that day, meticulous catalogues of flora, sounds of children, time real and imaginary, the quality of sunrise, the brilliance of a yellow warbler's backside dipping across his path to alight in an aspen he'd never noticed. His brother sat at the sushi bar, reading his letter,   scotch on the rocks, writing notes for a reply on bar napkins.

The image of man has eyes, Bolzebados wrote during the first weeks of his life in that room. *And perhaps*, he continued, *that image has an eye too many   whereas man himself has light*. This is typical but also insane. In his journals he refers to this time in the one-room studio overlooking the Plaza Santa Lupe as his surrender, a period where he only wrote what came to him, only what was given to him, only slept when he felt compelled. It was here he wrote the majority of The Book of Transparencies. As he wrote he noticed how his mind had taken over his body and he was no longer light but heavy. It was a constant turning of one entity into another as if surrounding each real thing there was a shadowed aura as alive in the ether as what was present before his eyes. In the end he was at a loss to keep these two separate and at some point he realized the futility of the attempt. This was when the shadow world overtook him. He slept extraordinarily late. Often on Thursdays when she was scheduled to arrive, the cleaning woman woke him with her insistent knocking. She had a bosom that had nurtured many children and thick worn hands but still strong. Time to get up Mr. Writer! in a broken Lithuanian accent, you have many words to get out of you today. Bolzebados groaned and she poked him with her broom until the kettle whistled and she poured tea. First you eat eggs, she said,   then you tell me dreams. Bolzebados sat up in bed, peeling the shell from a hard-boiled egg, speaking of the previous night's dream. He was plagued by night terrors, sometimes waking in a terrified state in the middle of the night, unable to pinpoint either the source of his fear or the nightmare's content. I do not understand it, he said to her. In the middle of scouring the dishes left in the sink from a week's worth of solitary subsistence, she shouted over the din of water. Of course you don't understand. The possessed never know they are possessed, she said. You are haunted and you will remain haunted until you exorcise your demons. That is why you must get out of bed and sit at that desk and don't stare too long out the window. The fountain isn't going anywhere. I will be back next week. And, with that, she left but not before ripping the covers off Bolzebados's bed with him still in it, then opening the window to the chill morning air.

✻

when were you most happy?

was it when you were in Naples and you had just bought the used green bicycle and you rode it   barely peddling around the plaza with the wind streaming from your face?

so you locked your bike to a rack near a well-lit parking lot in the morning it was gone

was it when you were driving down Eldridge Avenue in the stolen Chevy Impala   windows rolled down to the warm night   that slow sad song on the radio like a rain shower?

you wanted to get caught   but you never did

to write a book that would stay forever closed   is this futility? the image rises to mind shipwreck consciousness falling to the bottom of the sea   sharp cracking of wood tall masts tumbling into waves   to imagine Royston's thoughts the moment his body smacked against the water to imagine the havoc of that death and its grim appeal[1]

❁

He had to get up unusually early and hence took along into his dreams the delicate face of his grandfather's watch ticking on the nightstand. Childhood   a black happiness spoken through a piano   glimpses of evening skyline that undulated between Columbus and Cleveland and the violet expanse of Lake Erie at twilight   a locomotive working rapidly with its elbows   trees appearing in groups and alone the blue dampness of a ravine shuttling over his flesh   ambient and chilled in the early morning. According to the last entry in his journal, he planned to take the ferry to Peaks Island in order to make a more detailed map of the Battery than was provided him. He mentioned multiple times that he wanted to write a history of Sacred & Profane, the collective art festival that took over the burnt-out Battery every October. His history would create a fictional archive of characters and events that never occupied the actual festival but would lend

1 Steven Royston was a historian who wrote a history of the Great Storm of 1913 that sank eight ships on Lake Huron. In 1935, he was accompanying the crew of the Gray Goose when she sunk into Lake Huron during the annual October maelstrom whose twenty-five foot waves swept on-lookers from the black rocks out into the lake. According to accounts from Royston's wife he had finished the majority of his work on the book and had brought his only manuscript on board the Goose to edit during the voyage. It is my belief that a very prominent portion of Bolzebados did not want to ever finish The Book of Transparencies. In fact when he disappeared off the back of the ferry to Peaks Island, Bolzebados had probably finished the manuscript or at least came as close as he could allow himself to admit.

a parallel invented truth, an intimate fabrication, to the Battery's ghost structure.

She was still beautiful, he thought, and yet solitude seemed to enclose her as vines enclose a garden. She lived alone, had almost no friends and for many years, she worked on sculptures in wood but neglected to show them to anyone. Each time she finished a piece she destroyed it and began the next one. Glancing beneath the table of the all-night diner, he noticed the contour of her toes, how the fourth one bulged misshapen like a marble had been wedged into the joint. Her pinky toe was a squat mass of clay. She raised her foot beneath the table onto his chair, placing her heel between his legs, letting the bottom of her foot and toes rest against his pants. He ordered another coffee. Cleo smiled and spoke, it seemed to him, in Portuguese. It would be impossible, she said, to say we are not haunted but how we live with the ghosts makes all the difference. He tried to agree but could only think of a rowboat adrift on a small lake without passenger or oars, cattails filled with redwing blackbirds padding the shore like cotton, waiting to rub against the rowboat, to soften it, and draw it in.

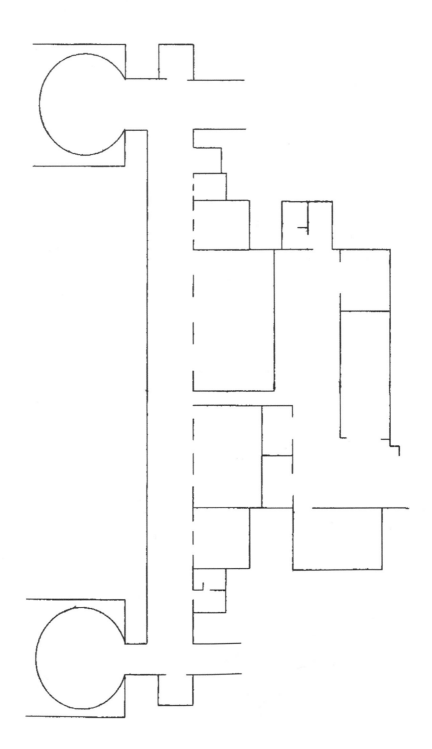

10

He remembered the spring not long after they met, one of the keys of her piano broke. F above Middle C. That season the two of them traveled to a remote part of Downeast Maine. He had been hesitant about the trip because he feared their relationship was not one that would survive an extended weekend in the wilderness but when she insisted he agreed, believing the trip would hasten the eventual. They camped near the edge of a sand dune that dropped off into the ocean. During the night, after cooking vegetable shish kabobs over the fire and making love among the black flies, he dreamt of jumping off the Seguin Bridge into the Kennebec River, his body tight, arms clasped to his sides   jack-knifing into the water. It was as if he awoke from a part of the dream when he entered the river but another part of him remained mired inescapably, though with a heightened consciousness, in the dream state. He entered an unfocused night and after several prolonged moments of struggle he resigned himself to the loss of sight but acknowledged the ability to breathe underwater. Encased in darkness he became conscious of Chopin's Opus 9 in E flat major that had been playing at a distance since he entered the water. It was played perfectly though somehow lacked a quality he could not name. He woke up wondering what was missing. It was dawn. She was asleep. He left the tent and went down to the water to listen to the sand fall into the water.

❖

who knows what would have become of me on Delancey Street? my fingers gripped tightly around the smooth rock in my pocket   eyes loose on the spinning sky   trying to recover from the onslaught of images popping in my mind   the way she lay fused on my chest as if swimming the smell of pine trees   the meandering strain of music drifting over the water   the churning Atlantic foaming teeth in the wake of the ferry   faint smell of skin beneath cigarettes I remembered nothing about my current self or my previous histories or anything else whatsoever I was told later I kept babbling like a large parrot in a string of incomprehensible languages who knows what would have become of me had it not been for the kind woman who looked in my journal as I lay prone on the sidewalk and found my name and address in Cleo's pleasant scrawl she had written my name and address to remember it and so that I could be found

when I collapsed on my way to the kiosk at the end of Delancey Street striking my head against the edge of the curb   I was taken to Bellam Psychiatric Hospital and found myself in one of the men's wards when I returned to my senses the elapsed time felt more like an indefinite period of years of which my only recollection was a vaguely craven sense that I had somehow lived a full life of eating and drinking   travel and fornication   but had burned through that life like scattered bits of hot ash through newspaper I felt with certainty that I had escaped the various prolonged sojourns of unconsciousness belonging to that disparate life   late night hours of addiction bolstered deceptively by sporadic lovers   all laced with a pervasive depravity my escape from that vision felt miraculous oil separating from water as if I was pulled out by the scruff of my neck my awakening in Bellam was a reincarnation within which it took months to recover enough to again occupy the world at large   I walked around Bellam's grounds   my body stiff and fibrous left hand in constant touch for balance with the asylum's outer brick wall   in a distant state of mind   barren and yet vacantly content   I wandered   wrapped in a worn pea coat and skull cap given to me by one of the hospital wardens   for hours over the soft earth of the hospital cemetery   feeling nothing but the white-washed walls of my mind and unconsciously cataloguing bird calls   later when my mental functions and curiosities returned   I took to recording these calls phonetically in a journal and I also began prolonged stints in front of a telescope lent to me by the same kind warden   watching foxes run wild in the cemetery   on the morning I was to finally leave the hospital I saw two foxes playing on the shore of the small lake along the eastern edge of the cemetery   something was in the air that morning   the animals were stir-crazy hundreds of geese circled the pond   honking forlornly some landed with a smooth rappelling on the surface of the water

the M'Finda Kalunga Community Garden on Chrystie Street was created on the approximate site of an African American burial ground   as we crossed the east side of Chrystie and passed onto the extended median that housed a small soccer pitch and basketball court in the midst of traffic   we noticed   on that September Sunday M'Finda Kalunga was having an open house   a rarity for the garden   a small collection of aging men in lawn chairs congregated near the entrance   two of them immersed in a chess game on a stone table with the chessboard etched into the tabletop   a ceramic white rabbit lay haphazardly in the bushes behind them   we walked into the garden and the air became softer   we discussed the origins of the

word canopy from the Greek konopeion meaning   couch
with mosquito curtain   and subsequently from konops
meaning   mosquito   you pointed to the Sunday light
dappling through the quivering leaves   I asked you what
kind of tree was in front of us   the one with the thin
peeling bark and maple-like leaves   London Plane   you
said   especially tolerant of pollution and root compaction
especially suited for city life   we rested for a while on
a wooden bench whose planks sagged under our weight
you sat near me   almost touching   and I felt as if this
was our death   we had both come to the end of our lives
and this quiet walk through the burial grounds marked a
stoppage I had a vision of your mouth hovering like a bee
at the level of my chest   and I realized our relationship
was nothing more than a network of stoppages   brief
forays towards timelessness that had been unable to
sustain themselves a hummingbird flitted from one bush
to another and you silently pointed to the rabbit nestled
among the ground foliage not ten feet away   casually
watching us before loping off into thicker life I remarked
that it hardly seemed possible   as we sat in the middle of
this city in a neighborhood infamous and celebrated for
its noise and filth   that animals could move so slowly
without a trace of anxiety in their eyes how long could
we have remained seated on that bench? was it necessary
for us to walk through the tiny rivers of mud made by
the gardeners' hoses   past the birdhouses and white
rose bushes   and back into the city? did we have to
walk down the Bowery   south to China Town with its
mushrooms dipped in red dust as large as human heads
dragon star fruits   the chaos of Canal Street? was all that
necessary? was it necessary to injure ourselves again in
our attempts for more networks? did you have to return to
your job? did I have to return to my temporary home? we
descended the stairs of the subway   stood talking on the
platform for what seemed like an hour but was probably

closer to fifteen minutes   when we embraced you threw
your body into mine and I could feel your small breasts
press against my chest as you lifted yourself onto your
toes   my arms fit beneath your ribs   I wanted to kiss your
ear but my lips only found a spread of hair   I kissed that
nameless spot   we let go of each other and embraced again
I wondered if there had been a mirror over your shoulder
where my gaze rested for a moment   would I look into it?
you left for a northbound train and I descended the stairs
deeper into the station where the compressed odors of the
underground engulfed me

❈

In the background of her painting, beyond the trees
and the twin domes of the monastery, he saw the tip
of mountains, a small section of city, and a faint line of
river connecting the two. The city, an indefinable shape,
hunched gray, a kind of crust at the base of the mountain,
and above the mountain, the sky occupied more than half
the entire painting rain hanging from clouds. He thought
of her breastbone somewhere in the desert outside that
city, faintly rising, exquisite, a small flat stone in a river
that will some day be swept to the shore, only to be
skipped again across the surface of the water, to enter
again into agreement with the current but with no chance
that it will ever again slip smoothly between his fingers.
It was this surge of incapacity that he spent so much of
his life fighting against, trying to allay its crush-and-press
consensus.

Each time she finished a piece, she destroyed it. She did not want to keep anything she made or perhaps nothing she made wanted to remain. The destruction of each piece was a liberation, a setting free of spirits that would be happier in other less tangible worlds. The only record of her work from that time was her book of transparencies. After they'd separated, Bolzebados visited her from time to time in her studio in the White Mountains with a view of Franconia Notch. She once told him   as he sat in a caned chair amidst the sparse suspension of her work   drinking black coffee she had made especially for him, that once returning to the base of Mount Washington, after ten hours of hiking   she had to run down the last tenth of a mile to the trailhead because her legs had given out and were shaking so badly. She squatted over a small square canvas and he noticed the pure strength in her body, especially in her legs that had been made to be fast and strong. She poured wax   added ash from her woodstove to the canvas. Onto this base, when it dried, she added black paint, white paint, a few hints of sky. Bolzebados recognized, in the excrescence, the hulkings of a mountain. She called the painting Snow on Black Head and before she destroyed it she placed a thin nearly transparent sheet of paper over its crust and   with charcoal, traced its contours, rubbed its essence. She added this page to the growing book of other such archives held between heavy stock cream covers, bound with red ribbon stitched like eyelashes across the spine and all wrapped in a thin leather sleeve. Bolzebados noticed his breath rolling in white wisps. He wondered what, if given the opportunity, he would ask the mountain. She put another log into the stove. But perhaps it doesn't matter, he thought, I run in circles   constantly climbing, but the mountain doesn't care. Fires can burn the base, move up toward the tree line, but up at the summit, where she makes her own weather, it remains eternal crags and snow. He watched the way her legs moved in her paint splattered jeans, the way her hips strained at the seams when she squatted to shove wood, the small of her back emerging from beneath her grey woolen sweater. Years later, in a nameless café, as he sat drinking a pot of dazhang mountain green tea   Bolzebados encountered a former teacher, a woman he always thought of as a golden orange. Upon hearing of Cleo's book of transparencies, its physicality and assemblage, she said, this will become a book. You must take the responsibility to record it. You must write it.

Walking north on Vanderbilt, past the Roosevelt, to Forty-Seventh Street, turning west, he thought of mapping all his meandering steps in a single atlas of his life. A simple black line never ceasing to leave a mark   the tip of the instrument never lifting from the paper, tracing all movement from his birth to these steps along the pavement in the shadow of the Mercantile Library. This line created his body, black markings as residue, shavings, whiteness in between and around the line, the infinite amidst a ball of packed yarn. Every river traces the curves of a woman's body. If he were to make a transparency of this map and lay it upon the contours of another's body, what would arise? The subtle lift of a breast, the veins along the back of a hand, a down turned nose, chaotic crosshatchings over a palm? What would overlap? Would it all become clear in an instant? Would there be a corresponding mark on each thumb pad? He thought of Borges creating his own face from a lifetime of writing and he thought of his own childhood game of naming animals in clouds, birds leaving white imprints on his eyes. He entered the Mercantile, ascended to the second floor reading room and sat at a roll-top desk where he could look out the plate glass window into the street below with its flood of suit gray and pinstripe. The window reflected his face, beyond it, the city, returned him to the Bibliotheque Nationale and the several times he witnessed, from his seat in its reading room, birds confused in the library's forest courtyard flying into mirror images of trees in the reading room windows, striking glass with a dull smack, and falling with a lifeless thud to the earthen floor, their once constant tremors, whether from fear or desire, truncated.

In a letter, postmarked from Paris, to Cleo dated 17 September 1972 Bolzebados wrote—*once I dreamed of returning to the stone quarry on the far side of the river it was fall and I was hillside struck by the burning riparian colors I felt as I often do during this season the evidence of the living was to soon turn south vanish when my back was turned leaving me to suffer in her wake I do not understand autumn her sweeping ocher and eternal return always alarm me but I am not in principle against alarming things time is nothing more than mark making an act that creates so much inherent white space so many ghosts in its interstices these specters watch us struggle and could even assist us but they decline I have made too many marks and I have begun the process of erasing them* Bolzebados stuffed a book of half-used matches from Café Esperanza into the envelope. On the inside of the flap he drew a tiny chain of birds tattooed around an ordinary wrist.

＊

in the room above Plaza Santa Lupe I sat at my desk   a
woman in a muslin skirt rode by the fountain on a bicycle
I broke the crusty loaf from the bakery on the corner
spread raspberry jam and collected the crumbs in my
hand Cleo once told me of an act of prophecy for which
one gathers together crumbs in one's palm   shakes them
three times and throws the crumbs like dice she told me
this determined one's husband   I drank my cappuccino
I wanted to add sugar but had run out   I watched my
landlady cross the plaza   stepping carefully on the
cobblestones like they were ice   in the distance I heard
the cathedral bells of the White Chapel tolling the mid
morning hour   young children ran in navy blue shorts
accompanied by women in dark skirts and white blouses
somewhere   down one of the side streets off Plaza Santa
Lupe   a boy yelled   fire on the mountain   his voice
trailing off into laughter at the game he played with his
friends I closed the shutters and light broke into the room
through slats I lay down on the mattress   the only other
piece of furniture in the room besides the desk   and from
a shoebox   I took out a letter and began to read

＊

He lay on the park bench and thought about the time
when she appeared unannounced at his door with a pot of
borscht she'd made from her Polish grandmother's recipe.
He remembered turning her away at the door because
he had wanted to work, but called her back realizing his
blunder and she returned, wiping away her tears. How
she carried the pot that weighed almost as much as herself,

how she hadn't wanted to leave his apartment after they'd finished their bowls. They lay on the floor together, a few feet apart, staring up at the ceiling and talking of how they both wanted to live in the desert on a stretch of red dirt with a long house and a thin black river in the distance. At some point their hands touched and as he talked about the satisfactions of splitting wood, she wriggled closer to him. When she began to speak about night in the desert, their shoulders touched. That night as they lay together she saw the spirit of a crazed man with a salt and pepper beard hovering above the window to the avenue. She lay awake for almost an hour after the vision, turning fitfully, trying not to wake him but also hoping she would. Finally, just when the traffic on the avenue began to grow, she fell into a deep sleep and didn't wake until mid-morning to find him sitting crossed-legged in a chair drinking coffee and watching the sun slant through the one east window. Though she stayed a few other nights at that apartment above the avenue, out of an inability to convince herself to do otherwise, her spirit never fully felt at ease.

The man boarded the train for Berlin's Hauptbahnhof with a small worn satchel. The soles of his shoes were thinned. He had the look of a man who had been beaten by the weather. In his compartment he collapsed into his seat. Soon he fell asleep, his head resting against the glass of the window, a reflection of the passing landscape scrolling across his face. He dreamt of a blazing fire and the uselessness of attempting to control it. In the dream, the fire spread uncontrollably across the side of a mountain, and when the fire had burned everything it could, a squat old woman with sagging brown arms appeared before him with the most beatific smile he had ever seen and gave him a stainless steel carving knife sheathed in black with a white handle. She said to him, the only one who survives is the one who wasn't there. When he awoke, a band of six teenagers eagerly surrounded him in the compartment. When they noticed the man was awake, one girl asked him what was in his satchel. The man said, It's a MacGuffin. What's a MacGuffin? A device used to catch tigers in the Scottish Highlands. The girl balked there are no tigers in the Scottish Highlands! Well then, the man replied, this must not be a MacGuffin.

✿

Below us, we saw the hard and straight veins of track on which trains sped obediently into and out of the city like streaming opaque thoughts. From this height, I heard Bolzebados say in a distant voice, I always had the impression that life moved more silently down on the tracks though still in a relentless rush like the earth spinning on its axis that we never feel because we are in its midst. His voice continued, these tracks are the conduits of health or decrepitude, depending upon what they bring into or out of the city's core. I think I remember when I heard these remarks. It was winter and I was visiting the city, taking a hiatus from the one-room cabin in Ward, Colorado where I had been living for the past six months, working on my slim book, The Timetable. The book followed the lives of seven people, the number of the Kabalistic rooms of the soul, for eleven hours and thirteen minutes, the estimated time a passenger train would take to travel from Paris's Gare Du Nord to Berlin's Hauptbahnhof. I doubted if I would be able to finish the book during my allotted time in the Rockies and this lack of perseverance troubled me, as if I was fiercely holding to my presumed deficiencies as a writer, and my inability to finish the project was further proof of this point. As a northbound train sped beneath us, exploding from the darkened tunnel like cork from a shaken bottle, I contemplated what Bolzebados said about train as conduit and envisioned a freight train speeding out of my heart, headed for the outer boroughs, laden with my failures.

Before Bolzebados left Paris in late spring of 1972, traveling by train to Berlin, I envisioned him dilapidated in some café, sequestered against the wall at a single table. An aura of smoke lay around him as though he'd escaped but wished he hadn't and he knew that the price for his so-called reprieve would be a haunting, a hungry ghost continually trying to attach itself to his happiness. I could see his pale face in the beginning of evening as the lights burned warm inside the café's empty glass and chrome shell. Bolzebados was the only one in the café and from the vacant look in his eyes as I passed by the front windows on one of my night walks it was obvious that only his form was present, a simulacrum. The ghost had him and he was allowing it. Perhaps tomorrow he would bolster himself into an act of emprise, take a train somewhere into the provinces, walk across cobblestones until he forgot his pain body, but for now the ghost was eating him. I knew or at least I thought I knew what thoughts held him in their sway. He had locked himself in one of those quiet gardens in the city where nothing had changed for decades and it was as if all the events of his life, at least the ones that he thought truly mattered, Cleo, his visits to her studio, the small things he construed into a constellation of love, had taken place in that garden. Time as measured on a calendar fell away. The world inside that encapsulated space roared like a seashell to the ear. Bolzebados had an appointment in the past that he had to keep, for sometimes a risk is in the form of a return to something, some feared place, some idea or loss, injury or question. I wanted to turn around,   enter the café, take him by the hand and lead him like a small child, out into his life, to smell and taste the salt of the city, but instead I continued walking for I had my own appointments to keep.

When she left New York in 1970, she found a studio in northern New Mexico where she grew more and more distant, deliberately turning away from modern life, living alone, sending and receiving letters   talking to her one toothed Himalayan cat named Come Here (pronounced Kamir).   In her painting, Los Cordovas from Above, the city becomes a series of incidental vertical strokes of color, as if she had decided to paint the scene, then half way through, changed her mind and no longer wanted the semblance of a town, instead wanting to watch the landscape form around her brush.   A sketch poem from that period folded into the book —

> I take tones from the earth
> spread clay thick upon canvas with palette knife
> push against the fabric skin
>
> Red hills rose, blue sky cobalt
> pale green, cloudy and very cool

white cliff
violet hills shadowed
very black

trees
beneath gray hills

slender crow

The sky is different
The wind is different
The air is different

Some red hills

Even after her move to the ranch that became her last home, when the demand for her monumental works that she had made in New York significantly decreased, Cleo continued in the same vein. In the end   her ranch was so crammed with her sculptures that there was scarcely room for Cleo herself. Death, or so the obituary claimed, caught her in the act of soldering a brass wing to the back of a ten foot tall kitchen chair. The posthumous interest in her work has been moderate, with signs of rising critical acclaim. The final auction at her ranch found homes for nearly one hundred of her pieces, from the monumental to the miniature, and raised nearly four hundred thousand dollars for the Children's Welfare Center, a cause to which Cleo had consistently donated money and had, for fifteen years, served as chocolate chip cookie baker for the annual Fall Carnival.

At a certain point in our conversation, upon my request to see where Bolzebados did his work, the reference librarian took me into the sub-basement where microfilm that had yet to be digitized was stored. A trembling halogen light infused the contents of these modern caves and also emitted a constant low-level buzzing that began to fry my nerves after ten minutes. The librarian, who appeared to be in his mid-seventies and had been at the library since he was twenty-four, told me Bolzebados spent hours down in this labyrinth, researching the history of the city's subway or bridge construction, the Memorial Bridge over the Piscautaqua River. Sometimes, the librarian said, Bolzebados proceeded in a manic state, practically running through the collections   pressing buttons for the moveable stacks and shifting his weight impatiently for the stacks to completely open and for the light to snap on. Other times, he sat over one large tome for a half a day or more   his elbows sunk into a table, head in his hands, turning a page or so an hour as if drugged or caught in sleep. It was difficult for me to picture Bolzebados down in the bowels of the building amidst such flickering light. I felt him in this subterranean world at such a pale and faint frequency that I could only encounter his trace, the majority of his being residing in another dimension. Over the years, the more I traced Bolzebados's peripatetic wanderings from country to country, from mountain to asylum, from object to archive, the less this perception surprised me, for such is the character of a shape-shifter, a ghost whose location has already changed by the time one imagines to have pinpointed it.

a book on train wrecks by Robert C. Reed   a book of
South American plants   a history of the New York
subways   labor movements in Italy   a map of the
mountains a map of the desert the white mountains the
fire mountains that do not exist how to build a rowboat a
three volume biography of Proust leather bound journals
a small community college library a wooden chair Man
Overboard procedures   an Italian author   a German
author   a Czech author   a Swiss author   an Argentine
author   a Norwegian author   an American expatriate
come home to seclusion in her West Village apartment   a
series of sonnets about the places she has lived that must
each include   weather and trash   a recipe for borscht   a
box cutter a piano a hummingbird a fox a goose a seal
thoughts and further movement toward the interior

When he awoke on the 17th of October 1975, he knew it
was still the extreme hours of the morning by the opaque
light seeping through his windows. The resonance of an
airplane on its red-eye descent. As he walked through
the fog, he glanced east in the direction of the cemetery.
The sky was gray but had begun to show a hint of pink
and blue. He descended the hill to the waterfront where
shrouded men moved with steaming coffee and a diner
shone with a religious glow. He walked the cobblestones
of Wharf Street then crossed Commercial with his hands
in his pockets, bought a coffee and a ticket for the ferry.
Twenty minutes remained before the ferry's departure so
he walked through the piers. A lean black cat cleaned
herself on a dock then gracefully leaped amidst the
weathered support beams and vanished. He passed a
lobster boat left idling without captain or passenger and

thought about the boat making its slow journey out of the harbor and into the fog of the bay where it would be impossible to see any more than ten feet beyond the bow, head lamps ablaze, reflecting back a white wall.

✻

in the desert   where the light is clean   I work   all I want to do is work   I feel like I am speaking about a nun happy in her monastery

I came upon the following entry from one of my earliest journals another person must have written it   which is truth and melodrama   I want to burn it but that doesn't feel quite right   so instead I copy it here as an act of deposition

> William came to visit me. War floated in the newspapers. We spent six days in bed, drinking coffee then wine in our underwear, interrupting the peeling of an orange to make love, ten o'clock in the morning. White light through sheer curtains. Sheets always cool. We touched each other constantly, smoking cigarettes, eating kiwi fruit on the landing outside my apartment, still moist and a little sore after love. I knew the moment I became pregnant. There was the life I had been living, love and the back of his neck, and then it was all different. I am always twenty-one years old.

I am a place where things come together then fly apart fields disappearing into distant hills

It was on the same day that the woman I would come to know as Cleo who was also working in the reading room and must have noticed my growing melancholy pushed a note beneath the green reading lamp asking me to join her for a cup of coffee I didn't stop to reflect on the nature of her gesture and in fact I had difficulty pulling myself out of my self-constructed miasma if architects want to strengthen a decrepit arch they increase the load that is laid upon it for thereby the parts are joined more firmly together   I nodded acceptance of her invitation and we walked down stairs past the reference desk and across the marbled entryway down the wide steps onto the avenue she lead me across a series of streets not taking my hand but leading me by pausing every few moments to glance back and make sure my lagging form hadn't been waylaid by a tree pit guard or a poodle we crossed into the west end of town stopping at a café bookstore named after the sea   Cleo asked me what I wanted to drink and when I couldn't decide she ordered me a cloud mountain green tea saying it will be good for your nerves she ordered a cappuccino with a shot of hazelnut we sat at white plastic tables outside the café dogs walked by I noticed Cleo's knee-high leather boots and the day started to become more pleasant a man asked Cleo to hold his baby while he fixed his coffee Cleo tickled the baby's belly and the little boy giggled one of Cleo's former professors stopped by our table on his way into the bookstore he and Cleo discussed briefly a new Djuna Barnes biography how it focused on the formerly neglected but highly fertile period of Ms. Barnes's later life when she lived in self-induced seclusion in her Patchen Place apartment eating nothing but crackers for weeks declining to speak throwing shoes out her window at Carson McCullers and writing stunningly sharp poems as they talked I noticed beneath the awning across the street a hummingbird.

Governor's Island houses a school for the deaf on the end of the cement jetty that juts into the bay I sat and watched the white wake of a speedboat   one gallant wedge of a sailboat   a cormorant's shadow body flying inches above the surface of the water   wings kicking up plumes on the downbeat I looked out to Peaks Island   waiting to catch a glimpse of the ferry   and I thought about his death   how it would finally arrive   and how he had to be its author   how he had to leave the rest of his life   the empty spaces to exist without him

a harbor seal peered above the waterline then submerged only to surface moments later a few feet away   playful in the slick blackness. the seal's path became a migratory shadow   a well allowing him a glimpse of his collective body   a body free of his old mind shackles   the body he would fully inhabit after the deposition of his physical body   standing on the dawn-darkened pier beneath a wharf light   he took his journal out of his rucksack   tore out a page and wrote a note

✣

17 October 1975
Dear CBL,
My action is not a personal gesture against your ferry
service. In fact I greatly appreciate your organization,
especially your congenial crew. I simply want to dispose
of my body at sea, to take in water and drift. I have always
wanted to drown, to know how it feels.

Yours,

William Bolzebados

✲

The small cottage on Eidre was full of candles and he
wrote in the early hours. The cabin, like his room above
Plaza Santa Lupe, had a simple desk and a single bed
but there was also a pot-bellied woodstove that heated
the cottage extremely well on cool nights. In the stretch
of grass in the backyard   Bolzebados kept a chopping
block, an axe whose ancient head kept threatening to fly
off during use, a hatchet, and an iron wedge, all of which
reminded Bolzebados of his father who used to chop wood
as conditioning for his life as a boxer. Bolzebados spent
many of the late mornings, when the sun was beginning to
warm chopping wood for an evening fire. In the afternoon,
he studied Davis from whom he was learning the emotive
qualities of water, and he wrote letters. It was a thirty-
yard walk from his front porch down to the water where
a paint-peeled white rowboat lay nestled onto the shore.
In the late afternoons, before dinner, he rowed out onto
the lake. This brief sojourn south to Eidre was a curious
move for Bolzebados because from all I could gather
from his journal entries, he was content in his haunting at

Plaza Santa Lupe and he was certainly productive. The only reason I could surmise for his three-week vacation to Eidre was that he must have sought a respite from the emotional toil The Book of Transparencies brought on him. Memory cries mutely for protection and we hear its pleas but would do better to guard ourselves against its plangency. Involuntarily, our hearts open. Birds sing on our pillow as we untangle ourselves. Quiet lakes absorb the sound.

❉

From the unpublished sections of The Book of Transparencies

a cat claws the covers of the still-dark bed   canvas leaning against the wall   pink and blue   your coat limp over the back of the chair   the same six songs over and over on the stereo until they seam into the fabric of the night-colored room   fog for your bare feet   a bookshelf for your sweaters   glass of water when you wake thirsty

autumn sleeps curled in a yellow bird's nest   winter waits and watches my hand climb her hips to turn off the night's switch   before the sun's quick eyes begin to show   while the day is still clean and crisp and unsure what it wants to do   my feet shape sounds on wooden stairs   out into the golden dying color

your folios rise from brown to yellow to burning red and bleed you back to carrying your trays in the black rooms   cups rattling on white saucers   shocking everyone most of all yourself   impossible beauty once touched immediately vanishes   your loneliness   a rich yellow   a mystical experience to be shared by everyone   work as the only remedy   the way your body is both immanent and empty of meaning[2]

❁

Upon Cleo's death in 2006, which I heard about through John Forrester, Cleo's gallerist in New York for whom my brother once worked, I flew to New Mexico. I missed the funeral by a day. It was held at Cleo's ranch that she'd bought with the proceeds from her first solo show in New York. I stayed in Taos and on the following morning,   I drove out to the five-acre ranch. The long house was surprisingly plain with its dried chilies hanging at intervals from the awning. It possessed a layer of quiet that was so palpable I hesitated to approach until I heard the familiar clank of a bucket and when I walked around the side of the house, I found an old woman, tanned and wrinkled from the sun, pulling water from a well. She was the caretaker of the ranch and had served in this capacity for many years, as well as nurse and cook during the last two years of Cleo's life. There was to be an auction at the ranch in three days to benefit the Taos Children's Welfare Center and the woman, whose name

---

2 Too uninterestingly self-concerned. Feels more like sketch notes on a painting than a satisfying poem. Have no idea what 'folios' are in the third stanza, and the rattling cups are obtuse. I'm sure, William, you also have no clue what they mean, but you're determined to include them anyway. I can hear your voice, "The consonants clink so well with the cups. Who cares whose cups they are? Not me." For a man who could hardly be more transparent with his emotions, you sometimes like an obscurity that even you can't see through. Why is that? What satisfaction does this give you? I think you're hiding when you do this, trying to hide behind language. You always did like mirrors as examples of misdirection. But I'm not going to let you get away with it, at least not with this one. Still, there are some nice turns of phrase – "curls in a yellow bird's nest..." "hand climb her hip to turn off the night's switch." The end is moving, of course, to me but I am anything but an objective reader. I remember that cat, those sweaters, that painting. But you must write for more than me. And yes, I agree that loneliness is a rich yellow color, or at least can be. What body isn't empty of meaning? Shells.

was Anna, was preparing the ranch for the auction. Anna wore long dangling silver earrings and took me through the stucco rooms of the ranch, interconnected like railroad cars. I was struck by the quality of the light through the many small square windows of the house, a rich tan light shading the walls I suddenly recognized as that which surrounds the majority of Cleo's work like a halo around a streetlight in fog. I told Anna this and she said Ms. Barnes had worked at all hours of the day   including late into the night   throughout every room of the ranch, but always near one of the many windows. Anna also said Cleo wrote everyday in her leather journal. I told Anna of the book I was writing about Bolzebados and asked her if she knew who he was. Of course, Anna said and smiled slightly in such a way that I knew I didn't need to ask further. Anna motioned for me to follow her to a drafting table directly under a skylight in the middle of a room that had obviously been a studio of some kind. Crates of books littered the floor, half emptied bookshelves against the walls. The drafting table and its immediate vicinity were remarkably clear compared with the fields of paper everywhere else in the room. From the edge of the drafting table, Anna lifted a mass of papers and a book bound in soft leather with a leather tie measuring about eight inches by six, and handed the disorganized bulk to me. For you to keep, she said. I tried to give Anna one hundred dollars for the book as a donation to the Children's Welfare Center but she refused to accept it. Later that evening, as I sat in the hotel bar until closing, I read through a few of the unpublished sections of Bolzebados's manuscript, covered with Cleo's handwriting and editorial marks, and it was there that I read the original book of transparencies, page after page after page.

❖

From the unpublished sections of The Book of Transparencies

they called the house a castle   lights in squares here and
there   I tried the backdoor   it was locked   through the
kitchen window   squash sat cold in a pan on the stove   I
walked around to the front door and entered   something
hummed mechanically   I walked up the stairs absence of
dog   I knocked on her door   leaves of paper spread out
across the floor   leading to her asleep   a book splayed
out beside her   I opened the book and began to read of
orange peels sewn together with red thread   in the middle
of night   I awoke within the book   I sat at a typewriter
and began to type   the keys clacked but she did not wake
I wrote for what I thought was hours   I threw most of it
away this was what I kept[3]

No woman adds anything to the sum of woman   yet when
I lick her ear   how much of my body's burden am I willing
to lose

I see the childish inhabitant in your sleeping face   the
imprint of a fern in the sand of your cheek   love as
anything against the neck

Shallow pasty breathing like fingertip doves ruffles from
your mouth You wheeze and I leave for the morning

---

3 Too slow in the beginning. Too much self-absorbed narration warm-up.
Boring until "I awoke within the book." Engaging reflective turn at the end,
but I don't think it's enough to warrant keeping it in the manuscript.

Fresh from the furnace of your gaze I cry out in disbelief but as I do
I realize my hands are filled with babies that do not belong to me

A natural history of love and war   with birds   of course are their bodies unbroke   are they made of silver   has autumn ended yet

My Plague-Carrier   My Insufferable One   the scuttling of crabs along a rock floor   the safety of your bed   small animals across our chests[4]

※

with one hand   she paints   the other hand strokes an egg carton full of babies   one by one   the babies fly up into the air and combine to form a man   she paints the man within a furnace   he is in the process of exploding   she paints small jagged flecks of vermillion erupting from the base of his spine

for the first forty days in the womb a child is given dreams of previous lives in flashes of lightning   the child will take on   as one always does when residing in another's house the other's thoughts and will be subjected to the other's

4 I know you love ghazals, William, but I tend to think it is not the form for you. They cater too much to your love of obscurity and disjunct. You do not need a poetic form that asks you to do what you already naturally do. It is like giving a Sunset the color orange as a Christmas present. Rather, what is it that a sunset wants? An ocean to reflect its ending light? A container? (definitely not) A photograph? (I doubt it) Daylight? An observer? (no again) The evening sky? The chance to do it all again tomorrow night?

rules   for this period   the child's face is a lake of fast
moving clouds

and if many times I have painted mountains it was because
they elevate me into the cracked sky   high above the
tainted earth and its bruising abilities   distant but clouded
with clarity   I have my own weather   high and illogical
divergent systems come together   rushing up the sides
thin air seeks refuge from its own scarcity   I paint my lack
holes   a thinness   my paper lungs   I paint my crags and
footholds   small bits of life   a handhold and below such a
steep drop   I paint clouds and wind and fine dust   myself
as the mountain   how did I get here

✻

From the unpublished sections of The Book of Transparencies

The angel descends into her paper universe   she sits at
her desk like peace among the instruments of destruction
I ask her why she looks like sand in the desert   she says
because it is so cold and I miss you   I embrace her but
know I cannot stay   do you love me   she asks   I slip
my tongue inside her   I want to eat you   I say with the
rolling motions of my tongue   I swallow and feel you in
my esophagus   in my stomach   spreading life force to my
appendages   I invite you   I say   please nibble on my arm
or my thigh as it has more meat   you will like my calves
do not hesitate to tear my flesh   it is a mutual process to
feed each other   I am handsome and you are beautiful   I

have to work   she says   other bodies are coming for me
you are powerful but it is best to share   I cry and wish
my tongue were sand   but I know she is right   the pain
washes and continues to wash me until there is no more[5]

the piano began the concerto   haunting   an abandoned
road that is tired of being a road but must be a road
again   followed by the bass echoing piano then straining
into its upper register before taking the melody   notes
individually skipping and rising into the round air of the
station's main concourse   the music stitched together in a
ribbon that arced and rippled around the firmament   the
constellations on the warm lime green ceiling gave the
impression that the music was coming from somewhere
very distant but still with a precise sound   the audio
equivalent of an eagle sighting a fish in a lake from
hundreds of feet in the air   there are rare times when I
am able to see animal totems   usually in expansive spaces
and with the aid of some type of music   and such was the
case on this occasion as I clearly saw a snow-white goose
flying in lazy but precise loops through the air of the upper
atrium   the goose seemed to be listening to the concerto
or was possibly created by the music and so existed in

5 Why is the concept of failure so hard to accept? Is there more work that
needs to be done? Then I will do it. Is it a question of hard work? Then I will
work harder. Is it the possibility of the air swallowing up my soul? Then I will
run faster in order to remain ahead of my pursuer. Is it the blue melancholy
that sits on me like your peace among the instruments of destruction? Then I
will tear it all apart. William, what happens if your book is a failure? What if
no one will publish it? If no one sees its beauty? Wants more from it, expects
it to be something other than what it is? But I think you knew all the answers
to these questions. You didn't care if you failed to finish the book; in fact you
didn't even want to finish it. All you wanted to do was be in its service – you
wanted to write it forever, to always be working on it. It was the writing you
most cared about. Have I failed you now in my efforts to edit this book, in my
efforts to publish what I thought you wanted? Actually, now, I see you may not
have ever cared.

tandem with it   for when the music ceased so too did my vision of the goose   high and illogical   as if the goose had known its own future and had fulfilled its contract upon meeting that future   as I climbed the escalators towards Vanderbilt Avenue   I couldn't help but wonder if one of the geese from the lake at Bellam had somehow followed me   if some vestige of that prior madness knew that I had not yet escaped it and an embodiment of that madness had been circling above me   waiting for an opportunity to alight on the lake of my mind   on that night I booked a flight from LaGuardia to Paris

gradually I became unwell on the train from Paris to Berlin a phantom pain spreading through my chest   I began to convince myself I was about to die of a heart attack   the conductor would find me slumped over in my seat while the youths chattered that I had been sleeping forever when the conductor shook my shoulder   my body would fall forward and my soul would slip the locomotive and fly over the mountains   among the crags and stiff wind I encounter the ghost of the Machado who tells me of his attempt to cross the mountains with his aging mother during a snowstorm to escape Franco's regime   he smiles slightly and laughs as he tells me how he died shortly after his crossing   three days before his mother   he grows somber when mentioning that he never saw his brother again   but I didn't die on that passage to Berlin   when the train pulled into the Hauptbahnhof   I rose from my seat   stricken and ash white   I knocked on the door of my friend Tomas who had recently written a play about a sinister doctor and his descent into madness that had been well received by critics but left most audiences puzzled   if not repulsed   within a week   after numerous excursions around the city for coffee and pastries and to discuss our work   Tomas convinced me to travel south and stay at his family's studio over Plaza Santa Lupe   he convinced me to write the story that had been on the horizon my entire life

❀

The Book of Transparencies was published in 1977 by Black House Press, a small organization working out of Brooklyn, Philadelphia, and Holyoke.   They published a series of experimental chapbooks and a few significant perfect bound books in the mid seventies through the mid eighties.   BHP folded in 1989 when one of the editors died in a plane crash on Martha's Vineyard, effectively closing the press.   My efforts to contact the remaining editors were mainly futile because they were unable to explain the exact circumstances of how BHP came in contact with the manuscript for *The Book of Transparencies*.   The editor who died in the plane crash had brokered the arrangement, contacting the other two to say she had received a letter from a woman that presented a manuscript from a friend who had recently died.   Would BHP publish it, the woman wanted to know.   After reading the manuscript, all three editors unanimously agreed to publish the book.

After fifteen minutes of circling, Captain Blackadder called off the search, and turned over the process to the harbor patrol.   The Aucocisco resumed her journey towards the island.   What happened when Bolzebados hit the water? Was he swept under the white wake of the ship? Did he struggle to regain the surface, suddenly sobered by what he'd done, cold sting of salt water slashing his eyes and mouth? Did he feel his body jerk and spasm, silver-blue overriding his mind, muscles conceding to icy water? Did he swim towards life or away from it?

✿

From the unpublished sections of The Book of Transparencies

Friday Night Grocery

Red peppers in the kitchen sliced thin   expensive   the anatomical heart

Rotted purple onions kept too long

Creamy garlic the color of flooring   the color of walls   stitched with spider webs

Broccoli flowers and I really like your company

Half-moon mushrooms in the basement amidst metal chimes hung from the ceiling that align at a single point to signal safe passage

Carrots and your eyes are so big

Brussels sprouts and I like to hear you speak your sentences as you write

Garlic skins peeled and translucent   even the thinnest layers   even the discarded

Knives of various size and sharpness   white handle   black sheath   and

I cut you off from the side of my body[6]

❁

2 February 1976
Dear Black House Press,

I am writing you from New Mexico to ask you to consider publishing the enclosed manuscript, *The Book of Transparencies* by William Bolzebados. For years he had been sending me portions of his manuscript, which I had been editing, from his various homes, the last one in Maine. Six months ago he jumped off the back of a ferry in Casco Bay and drowned. I have compiled his manuscript as best I can. I hope you can see its beauty.

Yours,

Cleo Barnes

❁

---

6 Even the memory of you is passing from my consciousness, though isolated scents and scenes still arrive at random times. Is this yet another failure, William? Have we failed again? Surely there are instances of failure here, lost moments between us. What is the nature of failure? Where have I failed you? Where have you failed me? In between, the failure of words and texts, inevitable, but do we still possess the desire to continue the failures, fail better, fail more completely, which is, in a way, to forgive. I still feel present with you, even within these pieces I choose not to include. (These failures?) As audience, I do not feel outside your text but a part of the poem. Is that because we know each other so well? No, I don't believe so, because now, honestly, we do not know each other, not anymore. Our personal intimacy is gone, but the intimacy of a reader remains. You've created an architecture in which I can easily enter, and perhaps stay for a long time.

A woman recalled watching a man of Bolzebados's description standing against the rail of the Aucocisco's rear platform. It was a brisk morning in October 1975 and out on the water the wind blew like February. Fog lay thick on the harbor and a major storm was predicted to hit the coast by mid afternoon. The woman thought it strange that a man took off his overcoat in such weather and carefully folded it over the railing. He grasped the railing, swinging his weight against it, rising up on his toes as if straining against the steel. The woman looked around the nearly empty upper deck for others who might be witnessing the reckless behavior but found no one. When she returned her eyes to the rear platform, the man was gone. His overcoat remained limp over the railing like a discarded sack. The woman, after standing in shock for a moment, began to shout for the captain.

The ship docked in the early hours of the morning. A man in a blue uniform came ashore and made fast the ropes. Behind the boatman, two figures in dark coats with gold buttons carried a stretcher upon which lay what looked to be the body of a human being under a red blanket. From the bay with blue lips, tangled hair, pale skin. Had he washed ashore beneath the Maine State Pier? Along the beach at Bug Light? Somewhere near the new cruise ship terminal? Onto one of the islands? Peaks? House? Little Diamond? Cow? Governor's Island? Death by drowning is caused by asphyxia, liquid entering the lungs. In all mammals, water colder than twenty-one degrees Celsius triggers the mammalian diving reflex, the body's energy saving mode that channels all efforts towards remaining alive. The reflex causes three actions: bradycardia, a fifty percent slowing of the heart rate; peripheral vasoconstriction, an inhibiting of blood flow to extremities in order to increase blood to vital organs, mainly the brain; and a blood shift to the thoracic cavity to prevent lung collapse due to increased water pressure. The breath-hold-breakpoint is the moment at which a body can no longer voluntarily hold the breath. Upon water entering the airway the larynx and vocal cords constrict and seal the air tube, a condition called laryngospasm. Drowning is silent. After a certain point, and this point varies between bodies, the fight for life ceases and death begins. As oxygen leaves the brain, a feeling of total euphoria blankets the body that does not even notice the lack.

As I continued to look around in his basement, lifting various objects for examination—a finch birdcage, scattered books, an old calf-hide knapsack—and wondered about possible provenance and history of these items I became aware of a presence hovering in the darkness just beyond the blade of light leaning through the basement window. I paused for a moment, unable to move because of the felt eyes from this penumbral figure. I slowly turned my head towards the presence, half expecting a six-foot seven-inch shadow man to leap upon me. After focusing my gaze, despite my uneasiness to do so, the presence revealed itself to be an old tailor's dummy dressed in a black pea coat of heavy army-issue wool. The coat hung so loosely off the dummy that it seemed to be slouching too tired to continue carrying the burden of sentinel over these few meager possessions from Bolzebados's old life. The coat's wool was heavily worn, almost threadbare on the elbows and forearms, but to its credit, it possessed the gentle sagging of a much used and much loved object that, while its days of function were now few, held within its folds many fine memories. If such woolen memories were to be rained upon, so as to activate them, they would exude his subtle essence. At the foot of the dummy was a manual typewriter, the portable kind that was so heavy the adjective hardly seemed apt. Its keys were covered with dust in such stark contrast to the black matte finish that it gave the appearance of a snow's dusting. After I'd left the basement, for weeks afterwards, I had visions of the tailor's dummy at work, typing maniacally with a severed nonchalance in the dull stream of light from the ground level window. In the typewriter was tissue thin paper, thinner than any paper I'd ever seen, and all the words, none of which I could read though I could clearly make out the letters, were formed from dust. I held my breath as I gazed hard at the paper, trying to read the words, but I knew that soon I would no longer be able to continue. Lungs burning, I would inevitably and with relief, exhale, scattering the delicate ephemera of words never again to be reconstituted.

❁

in one of the most beautiful parts of the city   I had a window from which I could see   beyond a foreground middle ground   and even a third ground of piled-up roofs a violet bell   sometimes ruddy   sometimes also in the noblest prints of it   a decanted cindery black   I thought it the bell of the cathedral whose rounded tone I heard when life grew quiet around my ears   in the dormant hours of the afternoon   the tone was covered so well by the clamor of the city during the rest of the day that one would think its hourly punctuations had ceased altogether the voice of the bell was not gentle but not loud and the bell became a symbol of a distant presence that I could never locate like a melody with which one has become infatuated but which one cannot yet fully make out I searched the city to find the cathedral of the corresponding bell systematically walking a grid as much as that was possible among the haphazard diagonal mash of streets in that area but to no avail beyond my admitted lack of directional proclivities it was a mystery to me why I never found the church a mystery that I am becoming confident I have solved I now believe the church never existed on a map nor even possessed a physical address its only summoning was for me and for me only through that one particular vista from my atelier window like a mirage presented to a weary traveler who desperately needed water and rest for me I needed solace a quiet place to rest in sanctity but I never found that in the city and I found it cruel that the window presented such an allure without the possibility of fulfillment it was only after a certain point following months of effort and searching and frustration that I realized the bell was ringing for me as a kind of toll marking the end of my time in the city and encouraging through its elusiveness my subsequent departure that would bring me unfathomable relief and ease

✸

The last to come into my compartment was a woman wearing a short black cashmere cap, not quite a beret but close. She was nearing middle age and possessed some of that subsequent grace, but had not yet lost the glint of youth. I immediately recognized her as the infamous Miss Djuna Barnes, the Paris expatriate of the '20's and later the West Village recluse of eccentric renown. As soon she sat down and settled herself into the corner of the car, the woman immersed herself in a book entitled, *The Banks of Bohemia: Paris in 1922.* Only seldom did she look up from her book to glance through the window at the passing landscape of forest and sky. I tried to come up with a pretext for engaging Miss Bohemia on the topic of her reading, some witty anecdote from my admittedly limited travels. Alternatively I also attempted to muster the courage necessary to simply speak casually to her of weather or geography, but none of my propositions felt genuine to me and I was unsettled by the degree of anxiety this sequence created. The more I spun my machinations, the more deeply entrenched the woman seemed in her book, as if she could subconsciously sense my quandary and further strengthened her invisible boundaries because of it. Eventually the forest valley opened out, and stretches of concrete buildings began to appear at intervals as we approached the city. Suddenly Miss Bohemia, without a glance in my direction, exited at the first stop of the outskirts. It happened so fast that I mercifully didn't even have the chance to feel guilty or mournful for the resolution of my conflict. Later I attempted to track down *The Banks of Bohemia* and, while I found books on Checking Accounts in the Czech Republic and Money Prophets in Moravia, I couldn't find any trace of the book I sought, nothing in any card catalogue or electronic search, and none of my colleagues had heard of it. I shuddered slightly at this discovery, but surprisingly it was not out of fear that I did this, but rather at the acknowledgement of my fate that this too would be a book I would have to write, not now, but sometime in my lifetime of accumulated tasks and responsibilities. Soon as the train passed through the metropolis, the snarl of buildings thinned out and uneven patches of grass began to punctuate the asphalt at an increasing rate until the holes of green and mottled earth became the landscape's majority like a spreading spaciousness had taken hold of the terrain and found a way to thrive and expand until the speeding open earth outside my window balanced itself strongly against the blazing strip of sky at the western horizon. Glancing backwards in the direction I had come, I saw, beneath a cloth of rich purple clouds, rain imminent, the gray city in a great arc of silence. I had exited that convoluted struggling mass and had the sense that I now found myself on a dark island in a white sea, a lacunae so large that it stretched wide across many seas, its own continent, peopled with air and motion and the muffled sound of distant waves that signaled anything was possible but nothing was guaranteed. Then it was over, the glare everywhere around me, flashing reticent visions of both black and white, and thankfully the train continued westward.

✿

the area   in which I finally chose to settle after a series of disappearances a remote area of Downeast Maine lacked the checkered layerings of the city   but the farmhouse we rented a few miles from town rang with the energetic vibrations of my elusive cathedral bell   when I started the fire in the woodstove filled the kettle for tea and ascended to my writing studio in the hayloft of the barn at the edge of the property   I felt the frequency of a congruity   like the contiguous lover I had left sleeping in bed that beyond feeling good in my belly down to my root   held me in its orbit with a gravity both scientific and amorous   lovely in its simplicity

how can I make love to you without your body? it is not
so difficult

during a summer of abstinence   I slip inside you as we lie
together in a small square room   I carry the movement
of my legs sheathed in the tuning fork of your thigh   the
bottoms of your feet   toes curl   angles in the room become
less straight   one more   overshadows the distance

your face   like a person approaching from afar   breaks
into the darkness of the room to tell me in a hundred
whispers that I do not have to do this   stay close to me
you say   always stay close

＊

Once Cleo began working in the New Mexico landscape
the scale of her paintings diminished significantly.
Just before she left New York she'd secured gallery
representation in Soho and a studio in Tribeca where she
had been painting twelve by sixteen foot canvases. She left
the canvases in Tribeca and when she arrived outside Taos
she began to produce micro oil paintings ranging from as
small as two inches square to six by four inches on tile or
wood which took her anywhere from four days to three
weeks to complete. Most of them were variations on the
landscape surrounding her ranch. Every several months,
Cleo packed a few dozen of these micros into a worn
leather satchel and carried them by bus to Santa Fe where
she sold some in the town square on Saturday mornings
and dropped off others periodically at a gallery. The
desert's hands striated her skin in visible ways. Pictures
of her early time in New Mexico showed a vibrant middle-
aged woman, robust and in love with the landscape. Later

pictures showed a woman moving into old age, a face drawn tight with sand, gaunt yet kind with an ascetic air. One such photograph depicted a ghost woman with ivory hair overexposed so that white swaths ripped the psychic fabric of her body out of which flowed a pure clear life force.

*

To be painted with
broad brush strokes

{the color of copper pennies}

{in crayon}
Loving
leaves a residue
of dust and inches

Red
Hills
of
Sedona

I make
with little hands
my house.

{leave blank}

the last time we stood in the hall   the last time she said
good luck the last time against all the first times   the
first time we spoke in a room the first time we slept in
a tent together the last time we sang as we cooked   you
turned over in the morning   your wool cap after a night
of rain   still rain in a soft patter on the top of the tent
and someone was cooking breakfast   grilling potatoes
coffee and bagels   sitting near the woodstove   someone
knitting socks   listening to Tom Waits   geese landing on
the pond   long silent expanse of house cat stretched out
on the table   we slept and rolled over and continued to
sleep foghorn every ten minutes against the rain   the last
time we put on our shoes together   walked across the wet
grass towards the cottage   the last wisps of smoke from
the chimney   brick red leaves across the ground and birch
trees   slender white fingers extending down from clouds.

✿

Where did Bolzebados go to school? How did he get
from Ohio to New York City to Europe to Maine? There
are gaps in his life. His life is a page where the white
space speaks more than the black marks, more space for
the characters to move, bird tracks across snow. The
book is not large or long. It is by nature a ghost work,
insubstantial in its ability to flush out what can never
be fully understood. To answer the question, yes, it
is a futility. Such is the nature of the archive and our
attempts to understand a life lived in interstices. Slender
with large margins, including various maps and Cleo's
drawings, published by a small press because few will

sense its potential, especially if that potential is only lightly sketched. My knowledge and experience of Bolzebados is intermittent, like trying to pick up a radio station that continually fades in and out of range as one walks along the outer bounds of frequency. It also seems that Bolzebados controls the strength of his signal, choosing when he enters this world and allows me to follow him. This is writing as waiting, patiently for the signal to be strong enough to sketch partial impressions. It is easier to channel Cleo. She is more generous with her presence but Bolzebados, as shape shifter, a spirit presence, is more difficult to channel, not because he is less generous or more elusive but it is his nature to maintain distance and to remain in motion, shifting his energy inhabitations. This is not something he consciously controls but rather simply does. I think the book is suddenly much more complete as a poetic work of interstice than I had originally thought. I am ready to enter and edit the rest of the text and see what is left to fill. These last few stages, while not taking up a lot of page space, may take quite a while to complete possibly years, as they will include the quiet and subtle acts of shading adding the bits and pieces that connect the text like ligaments allowing a leg to move. Subconsciously, I want this project to extend into years of fine-tuning and research, and yet, while there is still substantial work to be done, its content and scope are much more established, both in text and in mind, than I had previously thought.

As he stood in front of her piece, a mixture of wood and ash and wax in the shape of a rocking chair hanging in the Pullman Gallery, he thought about seeing her for the last time, her right hand on the rail, while the left self-consciously traced a sign in the air which evinced the end. The train pulled out of the station, sounding its whistle a number of times and eventually disappeared at an oblique angle into the landscape of cloud, some castle, and lake. After a while, her figure became indistinguishable against the train and then the train poured itself like a snake into the ground. The white wisps that trailed from the smoke stack marked the last visible threads of her presence and when they dispersed, she was completely gone. What did Bolzebados feel at the loss of such an unequivocal constellation who so dominated his night sky? I can only believe he felt a relief so powerful that its weight being removed from his person must have triggered the dissolution of his being. A body never welcomes this, no matter how much it is needed. What happens next? And after that? How does a person exist in grief to perform the day-to-day functions of eating, defecation, smiling at food counters, the silent stipulations of society's living contract? How does a body survive when loss has left its gaping holes? How can a text be read when it is riddled with such holes? What will the wind do to it?

❊

I don't know what it is about islands that moves me so greatly yet I know that I am not alone in this passion an island has its own logic its own rules   there is something profoundly romantic in an island's ascetic independence and also something deeply healing   a place where one retreats to heal holes   the dirt path climbed steadily upwards toward the top of the Battery and the subsequent view to the eastern shore of the island and beyond   the ocean   the wind   as usual   was brisk and the flame red stands of sumac were blazing in the wetlands that abutted Island Avenue   to cross these wetlands   one had to tightrope across a series of precarious planks placed in snaking succession across a mixture of mud and water simply the process of describing this landscape   to say nothing of experiencing it   initiates a healing process similar to a doctor's advice for a patient to take the waters at Riva   I continued to return to the island because I could feel   on a cellular level that it did me good   it was during these regular sojourns that I began to catalogue certain aspects   making small maps   larger ones   notations on birdcalls and generally scratching out an archive of the island

her presence   when we unexpectedly met on a street in the Old Port reminded me of a calm bird at the end of summer its time in the northern provinces diminishing toward migration   but who managed to absorb the intense sienna energy of autumn without showing signs of the tell-tale distractions that usually manifested in humans as a feeling of sinking dread   the energy of the encounter reminded me of another such meeting many years ago at the same time of year and though the specifics had their own currency   the season functioned as the medium for experience   it struck me that the nature of relationships that have their origin in autumn are somehow shielded from the vagaries of the other seasons   winter's desolation and solitude   spring's burgeoning but fleeting rush   summer's indolent expanses but are subject to an intense core heat that can become a long-fed strong fire   or at other times   can become too intense and burn itself into sadness and ash   either way the essence of the union is heat   a grounded deep core heat that can intimidate outside and lesser relationships barring their entrance   isolating and intensifying the falling energy so that if the relationship is able to last the embers of the initial flame can fuel its existence for a long astrological period

I was alone   but then after some indefinable point   I had a lover on an island and everything was different   all my years of nothing had come to this   she cleaned houses   ran a singing group from her small cottage and was learning to play the guitar   when we met she could only strum downstrokes with her thumb   we met at the Brackett Street Church in preparation for the annual island talent show   her name was Fiona   long-limbed and supple shoulders raised   arched   stretched skin across shoulder blades   I volunteered to help make soup for the talent show and Fiona was the soup coordinator in charge of making a vat of white bean and sausage soup and a vat of minestrone   after I missed the last boat back to the mainland   we shared her bed   not touching   bodies still smelling of sausage   in the morning we lay in bed until eleven   listening to the crows and talking about the ways we would like to die   I was almost fifty   Fiona was forty-four and smelled of cumin and cardamom

I began the process of knowing her body in the dark   at first I knew her feet   my arch curved against the gentle rise approaching her ankle   one night I knew the surprise of her bare legs   the loose patch of almost translucent skin around the front of her knees I discovered taut skin over her iliac crests so pointed I felt they might break through in a bone white split   pelvis and calves and thighs just beginning to fall   spreading into new forms   navel as if a crow had left a footprint upon her belly   I began to sense   as we lay together night after separate night   that her body's origins lay in the historical darkness beyond the ocean   beyond form   and that her current body's manifestation was nothing more than a transparent skin under which she vibrated   her silent self shining through visible shapes   leaving its residue on her arm   her ear   her coffee cup   her wool hat on the love seat when I descended the stairs into a morning that had no direction

Fiona tilted her pelvis to meet me and in my wet palm I held her eagerness and felt her center beneath the soft pattern of hair like mottled sand   her hand brushed across my chest   a magical vacancy in her fingertips tracing rivers down my stomach   I slipped inside her and began to swim in our parallel lives   so many voices speaking in my chest how can we choose   what difference does it make which kiss we recover   kiss and kiss again   or what strange power we conjure but never fully understand   the fabric falls quietly around us   diaphanous layers   one memory as good as the next   one of her bodies does not diminish beneath another   to enter into her house of knowledge   to feel its moist walls   is to enter a white multiplicity

                                      ✻

Dear Fiona,

Let me introduce myself to you. Let us pretend we have not innocently shared your bed. Let us be old fashioned and slow. My name is William Bolzebados. My father was a laborer from Argentina who worked at a box factory in Cleveland, eventually rising to floor manager. He was a small man with quick fists. My mother was a librarian and piano teacher from Michigan. I grew up jumping in leaf piles with my younger brother, sliding down lawns in jeans, playing wiffleball in the backyard where our cat left mice for us on the pitcher's mound. I grew up climbing trees and playing Batman & Robin. My father taught me to box in the basement with a heavy bag. I once gave my father a black eye when an inadvertent right cross hit his left cheekbone. I grew up practicing the piano for a half hour every day before grade school   my mother sitting next to me   ghosting the keys with her long slender piano fingers. I grew up writing stories in pencil on the coffee table as my mother sat at the piano with my brother. I grew up   fell in love and became addicted to a past that no longer serves me and now I, William Bolzebados, lover of small things, the person I once was, must die, and I would prefer to drown. I have read it is quite peaceful once one acknowledges the act is occurring and surrenders to swallowing as much water as possible. The sun is really bright, the air is really blue. The water tastes like fishes filled with wind. Will you help me? Are you my death come to greet me?

Yours,

William

Ode to Small Things

My mother's charm
of the Eiffel Tower
my grandfather's
pocketknife   an emerald statue
of the Buddha   my French dictionary
the size of a thumb.

You should write something longer
my brother says. No thank you
I'll end this poem here.

※

Those who encounter Bolzebados do so by accident, pull him off the shelf at random to browse his life but cannot later relocate the space. Amorphous engineering. One begins to wonder if there ever was a person, or if instead, he was a ghost that existed only in his negative capability, in the white space that surrounded him rather than in physical form. In such a world, one cannot find the body. The body must present itself.

I do not feel agile enough for my usual fictional tricks and maneuvers, my fake empire, half a world away. And even if I did, they would only be to my detriment. Sometimes this heavy sadness, I never know how much of it I should surrender to, how much of it is an appropriate reaction to melancholia, and how much of it is indulgent embellishment. Still, it remains no matter how parsed.

A silence lies upon the house, a crow somewhere in the morning. Some silences feel peaceful, expansive, full of hope for how the silence will fill, other silences are thick, the crow's nearby call has to cut through a heavy layer of fog, a sickness as thick as dust. A few lines a day, something beyond discipline and malady, but yet in this silence every word is weighted, and waited for. There is an undoubted beauty in this, but also a falling feeling in knowing that the world you have struggled so long to create is finally coming into being.

❉

it was an accumulated constriction of the throat and chest   when I realized that my life was hovering around its own destruction   on the threshold of an untold body vastness   the pull of the interior was stronger than ever I surrendered   I spoke and people disagreed   I acted and my friends rebelled against me   I was in conflict and that conflict defined me   when I fought against its force   its ridges carved me   change   an act of aggression against the self   I began to notice causalities   a torn poinsettia leaf on the coffee table   lovely harmonicas in the afternoon whole forests knocked down   conflict forced me to act pressed me towards a destruction of which I was the sole author and executioner   I made new eyes and fresh skin   I destroyed the thin harness around the neck   I made noises with my mouth   I destroyed the wake up and the jumping walls   I made ghost gas   watched it escape from a leaky pipe   I made language without touch   I destroyed the tigers waiting in the trees and the spiders in the corners of the station   I made singularity   I made throw away sounds and no one stopped me because no one could   it was necessary   I wanted to be a decent lover of all things I jumped and no one stopped me

＊

Fiona & The Ferry
    A Children's Book

Fiona Strong Oars saves William Fall From The Ferry.
She picks him up in her rowboat in the waters of Casco
Bay and takes him back to her island house where her fire
warms him and she makes him tea. He sneezes a lot.

{Who will illustrate this book?}

＊

A man has fallen. It is a Sunday afternoon and a man
has fallen from a ferry. He is drowning. What are the
thoughts one thinks when drowning in a bay? His clothes
swell with water. He swallows. Grabs at the ocean. A
man has fallen. The helicopters are coming. Other boats
will circle. The day is ending. And now the day has ended
and the man has not risen.

＊

my book will not survive   unreal and untested   the room
is darker than I remember   I keep reading   my book
has not been written   will never be completed   nor read
copies distributed on street corners

in the end   it is difficult to know what exactly one dies of   I planned and planned again my own death   I even thought to write a book entitled   *The Ways I Will Die*   a necessarily slim book of the deaths I found enticing   a sort of hypothetical biography of death   beginning with the young stunt bike rider   Kit Crockett from Wisconsin swept from the black rocks of Lake Huron during its annual fall mega storm   his limp lithe body vanishing in a crushed instant   as a child   and even now well into adulthood   I was afraid that I would be swept from the shores of sight and would one day wake up blind in a dark instant where dawn should have been   or perhaps it would be slower   an unfavorable prognosis with little black patches and pearl drops gradually appearing in greater accumulation before my eyes   blindness   not a literal death   but the figurative death of a sighted world held a certain romantic allure and terror at the same time   I am not alone in this   when was it that I first experienced the insufferable sense of loss so difficult to shake   defeat   blindness   suicide   decay   the slow yellowing of pages   day by day   hour by hour   with every beat and stop   one loses more and more of one's qualities   becomes less comprehensible to a material world the self and its shell increases its abstraction   my preferred way to die has always been to jump off a high structure preferably a bridge   into black water far below   I imagine the exhilarating but irreversible free fall sometimes before I sleep   the rush of air and adrenaline   and I imagine there comes a point in the descent when the falling ceases to be an event the body can fathom within its set of previous experiences and passes into a realm approaching alchemy where the body is waiting breathless along the void's edge to discover into what the soul will transform

when I ceased to try   I welcomed the peace I so ardently
yearned for   the release of the need   the biological
compulsion to do   I spent the last three months lying
happily on my back   one by one I carefully brought forth
the fragments   starting at the beginning corner   faint
images I didn't even know I still possessed   and moved
forward   the book slowly assembled itself in my mind
paragraph by paragraph   page by page   names and
numbers melted into maps and diagrams   border disputes
and cinematic operations merged with quixotic episodes
when I found myself writing in a language I was unable
to read or onto a page that remained perpetually blank   I
smiled   the book filled my head   some bits were missing
some I found and some I let go   my head became too small
to contain the contents   the book spilled out of my head
and filled the entire barn   still some bits were unaccounted
for   I looked for them and some of them I found   a few
the book passed through the cedar   out through the
hayloft door and permeated the surrounding hills   their
separate curves becoming united with my circular mind
the book unfolded like a thin film and melded with the
trees   some of them   with others   the book became the
trees   and birds and sky   by now I'd already died   death
by drowning   the doctor pronounced   the procession
began   no one noticed that it was autumn   I now forget
the time on the clock   but it feels less chronological and
more of a prayer

Create a map of impossibility

{Draw it here}

I could see an arc of coastal shapes far below a clouded
moon   hills with rare lights and a black calligraphy of
trees fringing the silhouettes of a jagged coast as the skiff
drew closer   the air began to carry scents of the main
land   indecipherable organic smells that   although I'd
forgotten all memories of this country   I recognized as
home I imagined ruined docks along a quiet striated bay
firs   and the letters I would write   how I would describe
the husky moon as it lay a silver carpet over the ocean   in
time we would slip within these velvet masses and watch
the waves reach for us   last night in my sleep I saw a
paragraph like an island on a white sea

"For one cannot change, that is to say become another
person, while continuing to acquiesce to the feelings of the
person one no longer is."
- *Swann's Way*, Marcel Proust

Coda

At least a year after I'd finished this manuscript, during the period when the manuscript hibernated in my desk drawer, gathering strength and confidence, I attended an auction for the estate of Dennis Overly of Delaware. There wasn't much of real value beyond sentimental appeal until   out of nowhere   there appeared a 1941 Olivetti typewriter used by Marc Chagall and later passed, to my surprise, to William Bolzebados on which, the auctioneer announced, he typed a portion of the manuscript for *The Book of Transparencies* on the island of Eidre. I could hardly believe my luck. It was like I was seeing a long-lost brother standing at a podium, speaking eloquently about some Shakespeare, oblivious to my presence. A feeling of overwhelm took me. I wanted to act   to do something — anything — but I was hardly able to think. Immediately a bidding war broke out. I foolishly attempted to enter the fray, raising my timid hand, but like a schoolboy trying to enter a pick up game among mercenaries, I was quickly brushed aside by the rising bids, and the thought of spending a significant chunk of money from a nonexistent savings account did not seem wise. The volley soon intensified between Chagall's great-great-grandson, a seemingly questionable character who continually enacted the will of "Poppa" while placing his bid, and a subdued woman, nearly seventy   in a dark hat and sunglasses who quietly met and raised each of the young man's brazen advances. The drama reached its climax when the young Chagall shouted, "This is family property!" and then promptly ceased bidding and commenced sulking. I found out later   through a series of inquiries, that the woman was a representative of the International Typewriter Museum in Amsterdam and she was prepared to spend any amount for the artifact. Did the object follow its destined collective path or did it fall prey, for the moment, to the vagaries of higher funding? I would've enjoyed the typewriter, if I had secured it   but would have also been more than a little frightened of its ghost   for as I watched it disappear behind the screen, I knew Bolzebados's presence was not one to be collected despite the allure.   In fact   if I did secure the typewriter he'd used on Eidre, I was convinced that one morning I would awake to find it gone, having sprouted wings and, like some prehistoric bird, flown into oblivion, leaving only a few droppings behind as a joke, the impermanent scat of possession.

Acknowledgements

Slightly altered portions of *The Book of Transparencies* have been published in *Bombay Gin*, *Omphalos*, *Slumgullion*, *Octopus Magazine* and *The Handsome*. Portions of the text have appeared in visual art exhibits at SPACE Gallery, drawing room, & SCENE: Metrospace.

This book could not have been written without the support and inspiration of Interlochen Arts Camp, Jesi Buell & KERNPUNKT, Alana & Joey Chernilla, Reed Bye, Scott Navicky, Kathy Hooke, Patti Feavel, Bhanu Kapil, Peaks Island, Rob Lieber, Casco Bay Lines, The Authors League Fund, my parents and family, and always and most and with the biggest love, Sarah.

Jefferson Navicky was born in Chicago and grew up in Southeastern Ohio. He is the author of *The Paper Coast* (Spuyten Duyvil), and the chapbooks *Uses of a Library* (Ravenna Press) and *Map of the Second Person* (Black Lodge Press). He earned a B.A. from Denison University and a M.F.A. from Naropa University. He is the archivist for the Maine Women Writers Collection, and teaches English at Southern Maine Community College. Jefferson lives in Freeport, Maine with his wife, Sarah, and their puppy, Olive.

photo credit: Joyce Sampson